What Day Is It?

What Day Is It?

Patti Trimble

Illustrated by Daniel Moreton

SCHOLASTIC INC.
New York Toronto London Auckland Sydney
Mexico City New Delhi Hong Kong

ISBN 0-439-30551-9

12 11 10 9 8 7 6 5 4   1 2 3 4 5 6/0

Printed in the U.S.A.   23

First Scholastic printing, May 2001

Gil was glad.
"This is my big day!"

Gil saw Ann.
"Ann! What day is it?"

"It's Monday," said Ann.

Gil was sad.
"Ann forgot my big day."

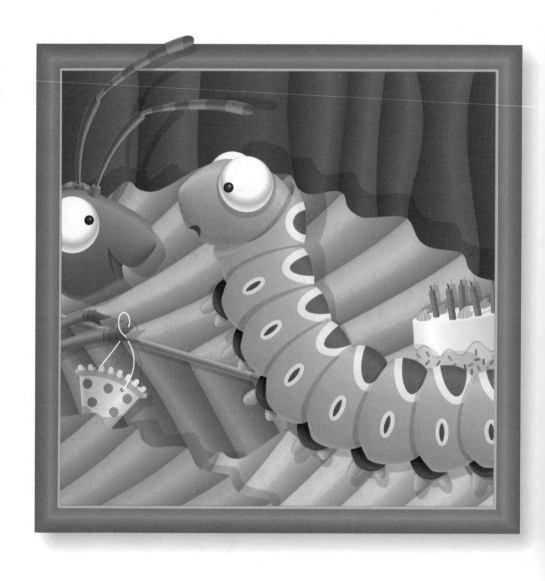

Gil saw Todd.
"Todd! What day is it?"

"It's Monday," said Todd.

"Ann and Todd forgot that
this is my big day!"

Gil was so sad.

"My friends forgot," he said.
"It's my birthday, and they missed it."

"We did not miss it!
Happy birthday, Gil!"

"Thank you," said Gil.
"This is a surprise!"

Meet the Illustrator

Daniel Moreton loved listening to his grandmother's stories when he was a child. They made him want to write stories and books of his own. He creates pictures for his books, too. He uses a computer to draw them, just as he did for this story about Gil the ant. He hopes his stories inspire you to write stories of your own!